*This LADYBIRD TALE
belongs to*

....

Chicken Licken

Retold by Vera Southgate M.A., B.COM
with illustrations by Lisa Fox

LADYBIRD 🐞 TALES

ONCE UPON A TIME there was a little chicken called Chicken Licken.

One day an acorn fell from a tree and hit Chicken Licken on the head.

Chicken Licken thought that the sky was falling down. So he ran off to tell the king.

On the way, Chicken Licken met Henny Penny.

"Good morning, Chicken Licken," said Henny Penny. "Where are you going in such a hurry?"

"Oh! Henny Penny!" said Chicken Licken. "The sky is falling down and I'm on my way to tell the king."

"Then I'd better go with you," said Henny Penny.

So Chicken Licken and Henny Penny hurried on, to tell the king that the sky was falling down.

On the way, Chicken Licken and Henny Penny met Cocky Locky.

"Good morning, Chicken Licken," said Cocky Locky. "Where are you two going in such a hurry?"

"Oh! Cocky Locky!" said Chicken Licken. "The sky is falling down and we are on our way to tell the king."

"Then I'd better go with you," said Cocky Locky.

So Chicken Licken, Henny Penny and Cocky Locky hurried on, to tell the king that the sky was falling down.

On the way, Chicken Licken, Henny Penny and Cocky Locky met Ducky Lucky.

"Good morning, Chicken Licken," said Ducky Lucky. "Where are you all going in such a hurry?"

"Oh! Ducky Lucky!" said Chicken Licken. "The sky is falling down and we are on our way to tell the king."

"Then I'd better go with you," said Ducky Lucky.

So Chicken Licken, Henny Penny, Cocky Locky and Ducky Lucky hurried on, to tell the king that the sky was falling down.

On the way, Chicken Licken, Henny Penny, Cocky Locky and Ducky Lucky met Drakey Lakey.

"Good morning, Chicken Licken," said Drakey Lakey. "Where are you all going in such a hurry?"

"Oh! Drakey Lakey!" said Chicken Licken. "The sky is falling down and we are on our way to tell the king."

"Then I'd better go with you," said Drakey Lakey.

So Chicken Licken, Henny Penny, Cocky Locky, Ducky Lucky and Drakey Lakey hurried on, to tell the king that the sky was falling down.

On the way, Chicken Licken, Henny Penny, Cocky Locky, Ducky Lucky and Drakey Lakey met Goosey Loosey.

"Good morning, Chicken Licken," said Goosey Loosey. "Where are you all going in such a hurry?"

"Oh! Goosey Loosey!" said Chicken Licken. "The sky is falling down and we are on our way to tell the king."

"Then I'd better go with you," said Goosey Loosey.

So Chicken Licken, Henny Penny, Cocky Locky, Ducky Lucky, Drakey Lakey and Goosey Loosey hurried on, to tell the king that the sky was falling down.

On the way, Chicken Licken,
Henny Penny, Cocky Locky,
Ducky Lucky, Drakey Lakey
and Goosey Loosey met
Turkey Lurkey.

"Good morning, Chicken Licken,"
said Turkey Lurkey. "Where are
you all going in such a hurry?"

"Oh! Turkey Lurkey!" said Chicken Licken. "The sky is falling down and we are on our way to tell the king."

"Then I'd better go with you," said Turkey Lurkey.

So Chicken Licken, Henny Penny,
Cocky Locky, Ducky Lucky,
Drakey Lakey, Goosey Loosey
and Turkey Lurkey hurried on,
to tell the king that the sky was
falling down.

On the way, Chicken Licken, Henny Penny, Cocky Locky, Ducky Lucky, Drakey Lakey, Goosey Loosey and Turkey Lurkey met Foxy Loxy.

"Good morning, Chicken Licken," said Foxy Loxy. "Where are you all going in such a hurry?"

"Oh! Foxy Loxy!" said Chicken Licken. "The sky is falling down and we are on our way to tell the king."

"I know where to find the king," said Foxy Loxy. "You had better all follow me."

So Chicken Licken, Henny Penny,
Cocky Locky, Ducky Lucky,
Drakey Lakey, Goosey Loosey
and Turkey Lurkey followed
Foxy Loxy.

Foxy Loxy led them straight
into his den, where his wife and
their little foxes were waiting for
their dinners.

Then the foxes ate Chicken Licken, Henny Penny, Cocky Locky, Ducky Lucky, Drakey Lakey, Goosey Loosey and Turkey Lurkey for their dinners.

So Chicken Licken never found the king to tell him that he thought the sky was falling down.

A History of Chicken Licken

The classic tale of *Chicken Licken* is a much-loved story. Also known as *Henny Penny*, the story of a chick who believes the sky is falling down has featured in books, films and even songs!

Walt Disney made two animated films about this intrepid little chick. The first one, released during World War II, was a short animated cartoon. Then in 2005, the studios released a feature-length, computer animated film, which brought the story to a new generation of children.

Chicken Licken is one of several lyrical stories that are often called 'cumulative' or 'chain' tales. The story relies on repetition and rhythmic text to progress, with an extra character adding something new to the story.

Ladybird's 1969 retelling by Vera Southgate has helped to keep the tale a firm favourite today.

Collect more fantastic

LADYBIRD TALES

Little Red Riding Hood
9781409311126

Goldilocks and the Three Bears
9781409311119

Cinderella
9781409311072

Jack and the Beanstalk
9781409311102

The Gingerbread Man
9781409311096

The Three Little Pigs
9781409311089

The Three Billy Goats Gruff
9781409311065

Hansel and Gretel
9781409311133

Puss in Boots
9781409311225

Rapunzel
9781409311195

Rumpelstiltskin
9781409311164

The Elves and the Shoemaker
9781409311188

Snow White and the Seven Dwarfs

9781409311171

The Enormous Turnip

9781409311218

The Magic Porridge Pot

9781409311201

Sleeping Beauty

9781409311157

The Princess and the Frog

9780718192556

Dick Whittington

9780718192532

The Big Pancake

9780718192549

Beauty and the Beast

9780718192587

The Little Red Hen

9780718192525

The Ugly Duckling

9780718193133

The Princess and the Pea

9780718192570

Chicken Licken

9780718192563

Endpapers taken from series 606d,
first published in 1964

A catalogue record for this book is available from the British Library

Published by Ladybird Books Ltd
80 Strand London WC2R 0RL
A Penguin Company

001

ISBN: 978-0-71819-256-3

Printed in China